C000155785

Tucholsky   Wagner   Zola
Turgenev   Wallace
      Twain   Walther von der Vogelw
                  Weber
Fechner   Weiße Rose   von Fallersleben   Kant   Ernst   Frey
       Fichte   Hölderlin   Richthofen   Frommel
       Engels   Fielding   Eichendorff   Tacitus   Dumas
Fehrs   Faber   Flaubert
          Maximilian I. von Habsburg   Fock   Eliasberg   Ebner Eschenbach
Feuerbach   Eliot   Zweig
              Ewald   Vergil
      Goethe   Elisabeth von Österreich   London
Mendelssohn   Balzac   Shakespeare   Dostojewski   Ganghofer
       Trackl   Lichtenberg   Rathenau   Doyle   Gjellerup
            Stevenson   Hambruch
Mommsen   Tolstoi   Lenz   Droste-Hülshoff
       Thoma   von Arnim   Hanrieder
Dach   Verne   Hägele   Hauff   Humboldt
       Reuter   Rousseau   Hagen   Gautier
  Karrillon   Garschin   Hauptmann
              Defoe   Baudelaire
     Damaschke   Descartes   Hebbel   Hegel   Kussmaul   Herder
Wolfram von Eschenbach   Schopenhauer
              Darwin   Dickens   Rilke   George
  Bronner   Melville   Grimm   Jerome
       Campe   Horváth   Aristoteles   Bebel   Proust
 Bismarck   Vigny   Barlach   Voltaire   Federer
          Gengenbach   Heine   Herodot
 Storm   Casanova   Tersteegen   Grillparzer   Georgy
       Chamberlain   Lessing   Langbein   Gilm   Gryphius
Brentano   Lafontaine
 Strachwitz   Claudius   Schiller   Schilling   Kralik   Iffland   Sokrates
       Katharina II. von Rußland   Bellamy   Gibbon   Tschechow
                          Gerstäcker   Raabe
 Löns   Hesse   Hoffmann   Gogol   Wilde   Vulpius
 Luther   Heym   Hofmannsthal   Gleim
       Roth   Heyse   Klopstock   Klee   Hölty   Morgenstern   Goedicke
Luxemburg   Puschkin   Homer   Kleist
       Machiavelli   La Roche   Horaz   Mörike   Musil
 Navarra   Aurel   Musset   Kierkegaard   Kraft   Kraus
 Nestroy   Marie de France   Lamprecht   Kind   Kirchhoff   Hugo   Moltke
 Nietzsche   Nansen   Laotse   Ipsen   Liebknecht
          Marx   Ringelnatz
 von Ossietzky   Lassalle   Gorki   Klett   Leibniz
          May   vom Stein   Lawrence   Irving
Petalozzi   Platon
       Sachs   Pückler   Michelangelo   Knigge   Kafka
       Poe   Liebermann   Kock
    de Sade   Praetorius   Mistral   Zetkin   Korolenko

CONTENTS

LIST OF ILLUSTRATIONS

COLOUR PLATES

BLACK AND WHITE ILLUSTRATIONS

CASSELL'S

"EYES AND NO EYES"

Seventh Book

ON THE SEASHORE.

LESSON I.

FIVE-FINGERED JACK.

What fun it is down by the sea at low tide! Scrambling among the slippery rocks, we quickly fill a bucket with curious things. Some are dead, others very much alive; but all have a story to tell us--the story of the life they lead on the bed of the sea, or among the sands and rocks of the shore.

Look, here is a Starfish! It is lying on the sand, left high and dry by the waves, for now the tide is low. The Starfish looks limp and lifeless, its five reddish-coloured "arms" are quite still.

We know it is an animal that lives in the sea, and dies when washed ashore. But what does it do in the sea? How does it move without legs or fins? How can it live without a head? Has it a mouth? What does it eat, and how does it find its food?

Like so many other sea-animals, the Starfish is a puzzle. Some of its little tricks puzzled clever people until quite lately. But we know most of its secrets now.

Pass your finger down one of its arms, or rays. It feels rough, being covered with knobs and prickles. Now turn the Starfish over, and look carefully at its underside. In the centre, where the five arms meet, is the animal's mouth. A harmless sort of mouth, you think, too small to be of much use. Really, it is a terrible mouth, the mouth of an ogre!

We notice a groove down the centre of each ray. But what are those little moving things which bend this way and that, as if feeling for something? Now that is exactly what they are doing. They are the feet of the Starfish. Each tiny foot is really a hollow tube, which can be pushed out or drawn in. At the tip of each is a powerful sucker, which acts rather like those leather suckers boys sometimes play with. Suppose the Starfish wishes to take a walk along the bed of the sea. First, it pushes out its tube-feet. Each sucker fixes itself to a stone or other object, and then the animal can draw its body along. You will see presently that the suckers can do other work too.

Our Starfish will die, however, unless we carry it to a pool. Before doing so, we must look at the tip of each ray for a small reddish spot. That is the Starfish's eye. Are those little eyes of much use in helping the creature to find its dinner? I think not. Most likely the Starfish *smells* its way.

If we put the animal on its back in a rock-pool we shall see the tube-feet at work. Once in the water our Starfish revives, and makes efforts to right itself. Can it turn over and crawl away?

The little tube-feet come out of their holes and begin to bend about. Now those near the edge of one "arm" feel the ground. Each tiny sucker at once takes hold, more and more of them touch the ground as the ray is turned right side up, and at last the Starfish turns over, and, slowly but surely, glides away.

COMMON FIVE-FINGERED STARFISH.

Stones, shells, or rocks do not stop it. The rays slide up and over them. If we had feet like those of the Starfish, a journey up the wall of a house, over the roof, and down again, would be nothing to us. Nature gives all creatures the kind of foot which suits the life they lead. And it is hard to imagine feet more useful to the Starfish than those wonderful sucker-feet!

Ask any fisherman what he thinks of the "harmless" Starfish, and he will call it a pest and a nuisance. "It gets into the crab traps," he says, "and eats all the bait. And when we are line-fishing it sucks the bait off our hooks, and sometimes swallows hook and all." Small wonder that Five-fingers, or Five-fingered Jack, as it is called, has no friend among fisher-folk.

On pulling up a useless Starfish instead of a real fish, the fisherman tears the offender in half and throws the halves back into the waves. By doing this he harms himself more than the Starfish! Each half grows into a perfect Starfish with five rays complete. We can say that each part of this animal has a separate life, for each part can grow when torn away.

If you were asked to open an oyster you would need tools, would you not? Even with an oyster-knife it is not always an easy job. The oyster, tight in his shelly fortress, seems safe from the attack of a weak Starfish. Yet the Starfish opens and eats oysters as part of its everyday life.

Finding a nice fat oyster, it sets to work. The Starfish folds its rays over its victim, with its mouth against the edge where the shells meet. The tug-of-war begins. The Starfish's tube-feet try to pull the shells apart; the oyster, with all its strength, tries to keep them shut. It is stronger than its enemy, and yet the steady pull of hundreds of suckers is more than it can stand, and the shells, after a time, begin to gape a little.

Now a strange thing happens. The mouth of the Starfish opens into a kind of bag which slips between the oyster shells. The Starfish, as it were, turns itself inside-out! It then eats the oyster and leaves the clean shell.

Mussels are smaller, so they are eaten in a different way. The Starfish merely presses the mussel into its mouth, cleans out the shells, and throws them away. Were we not right to call this wonderful mouth the mouth of an ogre?

Oysters, as you know, are so valuable that we rear them in special "beds." Along comes the hungry Starfish, with thousands of its relations, finding the fat oysters very good eating. They do great damage in our oyster-fisheries, and it is one long battle between them and the keepers of the "beds."

Supporting the tough skin of Five-fingered Jack is a wonderful skeleton. It is like a network of fine plates and rods made of lime. Perhaps you have seen one in a museum.

Five-fingers has a great number of cousins, some of them common enough along our shores. One of the strangest is the Brittle Star. On first seeing one of these animals I tried to capture it by holding its long, wriggling arms. At once the arms broke off. Then I tried to scoop the creature out of its watery home. But it began to break its "rays" off as if they were of no value whatever. To my surprise, the broken "rays" broke again while wriggling on the ground. This is a strange habit, is it not? Perhaps the Brittle Star has found this dodge useful in escaping from enemies. Anyhow, the loss of an arm or two matters little, for others grow in their place.

Another cousin of the Starfish is the Sea-urchin, a round prickly creature rather like the burr of the sweet-chestnut tree. This mass of prickles is not a vegetable; he is very much alive. Nature has given many plants and animals these prickles, like fixed bayonets, for a defence against their enemies. You will at once think of the gorse and the hedgehog, or urchin, as some people call it. Our little Sea-urchin has prickles, like the hedgehog, but he is really unlike any other living creature, except, perhaps, the Starfish.

If you were to roll up a Starfish into a ball, and then stick about three thousand spines on the ball thus made, you would have a creature looking rather like a Sea-urchin.

Beneath the mass of spines there is a hard *test* or shell, made of plates joined closely together; this is the skeleton of the Sea-urchin. Sometimes you find this strange shell on the seashore, rather dirty, and not always sweet-smelling. You might also find Sea-urchins half-dead, washed into the rock-pools. The shells are wonderful objects, so you should clean them in fresh water; they are well worth the trouble of taking home.

All over the shell you will see little rounded knobs. These show where the spines were fixed on; each spine fits into a hole in the shell, but so loosely that it is able to move about. The Sea-urchin can walk by moving its spines, tilting its body along from one place to another on the bed of the sea. It can do much more than that. Like its cousin the Starfish, it has numerous tube-feet, so you would not be surprised to see this prickly ball walk up the face of a rock.

The tube-feet, or sucker-feet, are fixed to the shell in much the same way as the spines. They can be bent this way or that. If the

Urchin is on a rock he clings tightly with these sucker-feet; then, if he wishes to move away, you will see the long thin tubes stretch out and bend about. They fix themselves to the rock, and the animal is drawn along.

TEST OR SHELL OF A SEA-URCHIN.

Besides these spines and suckers, the Sea-urchin owns another set of tools. Scattered over it, among the spines, are many tiny rods tipped with little teeth or pincers. You will not be able to see them, except under a magnifying glass. Of what use are these strange little pincers or rods? It is thought that the Urchin uses them in several ways. They may help in capturing small prey, or they may be used when the creature has to fight a larger enemy. They are also certainly of use as cleansing tools. That is to say, they can pick off tiny scraps of weed or dirt which settle on the animal's body. Some Starfishes also own pincers of this sort, but they are not so perfect as those of the funny little Urchin. We must not forget that all these spines, tube-feet, and pincers are worked by a set of muscles.

In the centre of the Urchin's shell is its mouth. The Starfish, we found, had a terrible mouth, but that of the Urchin is worse still. Not only is it of great size, but it is fitted with strong jaws and five long, sharp teeth, You may see them poking out from the mouth of the animal, and feel for yourself how hard they are.

There is a great deal more to know about Five-fingers; and the Sea-urchin still has his secrets which no one can explain. We have but glanced at their story in this lesson; but you can see that the Starfish, lying limp on the sands, is not so dull as it looks.

EXERCISES

1. Where is the mouth of the Starfish placed?

2. Describe how the Starfish moves.

3. How does the Starfish feed on the oyster?

4. Why is the *Brittle* Star given that name?

5. How do the Starfish and Sea-urchin keep themselves clean?

LESSON II.

A STROLL BY THE SEA.

The sea and the land are always at war. When you are at the sea-side, with spade and bucket to make "castles" and "pies" of the sand, you can see and hear the battle.

A wave comes rolling smoothly on towards the shore. It reaches the land and can go no further, and then, with a roar and a crash and splash of sparkling foam, it breaks. It spreads into a sheet of foaming water, and, after rushing as far as it can up the beach, it seethes back as the next wave takes up the battle.

What a grinding and tearing, as wave after wave is hurled at the land! That is the battle-cry of the land and sea! Most of the pebbles and the sand on the beach have been won from the land in the great fight. We might call them the spoils of war. Once they formed part of the solid land, the rock or cliff. Now they are loose fragments spread for mile after mile round our coast.

Every wave takes them up and has fine fun with them. Pebbles and sand are picked up, swirled along, and thrown at the shore. They are sucked back as the wave is broken by the land. And then the following wave takes them, grinds them and scrubs them to-gether. Thus they are jostled hither and thither, up and down the coast; and, as a result of the long, long fight, rocks and cliffs become pebbles, sand, or mud.

Now if you look at the pebbles on the shore you see that many of them are smooth and round. Some are as round as the "marbles" you play with. No wonder, for the mighty sea has scoured them with sand and rolled them for miles.

As you know, the sea is not always at the same height. It falls and rises. Twice in every day it *ebbs* and *flows*; we call this movement of the sea the *tides*. At low tide we can explore the very bed of the ocean. We can visit the homes of the living, breathing animals, which, at high tide, are hidden far under water. Between the high-water mark and low-water mark is our hunting-place. There we shall find the play-ground and feeding-ground of many a strange creature.

Here is a stretch of sand, with little channels of water; there is a patch of shingle mixed with numbers of tiny shells. The ebbing tide leaves shallow pools in every hollow of the beach, and these pools are often full of life.

Shrimps dart away and disappear in the sand as if by magic. Small fish and crabs hide from you as best they can. Helpless jelly-fish and starfish sprawl on the wet sand. What are those thin ropes of sand coiled up into little mounds? They remind us of "worm-casts." They are thrown up by a sand-worm, called "lug-worm" by the fisherman. He brings a spade and digs wherever he sees the sandy ropes of the "lug," for this worm makes good fishing bait.

Seagulls love to explore the shallow pools. You may see them walking solemnly about, picking up stray morsels. If you see a screaming group of them you can be sure that one has found an extra large prize, and the others mean to share the feast.

Let us walk down the beach towards the sea. Soon we find our-selves among rocks. Now these rocks are the bare bed of the shore, stripped of all covering. There is no mud, sand, or shingle, so here you see plainly the work done by the restless water. On every side you notice rocks worn to all shapes and sizes. Some jut out as sharp ledges. Others are flat tables, covered with a table-cloth of sea-plants. These clothe the rocks, or hang over the ledges like wet, shining green curtains. Nearly every rock has its crust of barnacles and clumps of mussels. If we are not careful we slip on the wet weeds, and get a ducking in the pools which lie everywhere among the rocks.

Here is the best place of all for sharp eyes to find the animals and plants we seek. Where the hard rock has been worn down into hol-lows, the falling tide leaves a pool of still, clear water. These rock-pools are the home of many a creature. So let us look for them, until the rising tide sweeps over the rocks once more, and drives us away.

Sea-anemones and seaweeds brighten the pool with their various colours. Pretty shells gleam here and there; and on the face of the rock there are more limpets, barnacles and mussels than we can count.

Where are the other living animals which we came to find? You will not see them unless you hunt for them in the right way. It is a game of "hide-and-seek." They are the "hiders"; and, as their lives often depend on their skill in hiding, you cannot wonder that they know every trick in the game.

There may be crabs, fish, shrimps, and others in the pool. If you look for a moment, and then walk to the next pool, your hunting will not have much result. It is best to lie down and wait patiently, gazing into the clear water of the pool. The little inhabitants are hidden in the dark corners under the rock ledges, or buried under stones and sand; or they may be hiding in those thick clumps of mussels--a favourite lurking-place; or else tucked away in the friendly shelter of the seaweed.

Knowing their dodges, you will soon become clever at finding them. Some seaside dwellers, such as prawns, are almost transparent in the water. Others, like baby crabs, are green or brown like the weed in which they hide. Even the sharp eyes of the seagulls must be deceived by this trick.

What a strange life they lead, these creatures of the shore! At times they are deep under water, and they form part of the teeming life of the ocean floor.

Then the tide falls and uncovers them. They are in the full light of day again, the sun shines on them. Most of them cannot escape to the sea, and so must face the enemies which prowl along the shore looking for prey. So, from one tide to the next, the rock-pool is like a prison containing prisoners of the strangest sort.

GULLS

1. COMMON GULLS.	2. LESSER BLACK GULL.	3. GLAUCOUS GULLS.

EXERCISES

1. How is the sand formed?

2. Give the names of some of the animals to be found in the rock-pools.

3. Where do these animals hide?

4. Prawns and shore-crabs are not easily seen; why is this?

LESSON III.

BIRDS OF THE SHORE.

On some parts of our coast we find steep cliffs, with the sea beating wildly at their feet. Elsewhere there is a sloping beach of sand and shingle with, perhaps, dark rocks showing at low tide. We explored such a beach as that in our last lesson. There are long, long stretches of sand and thin grass in other places, or else mile after mile of muddy, dreary, salt marshes.

Birds are to be found on every kind of coast. Some, like the Seagull, wander far and wide. Others keep to the cliffs, and many find all they need in the wide mud-flats. Such an army is there of these shore birds, that we cannot even glance at them all in this lesson. So we will take a few of them only--the Black-headed Gull, the Cormorant, the Ringed Plover, the Oyster-catcher and the Redshank.

Out of all the many kinds of Gulls, you know the Black-headed one best. If you live in London you can see and hear him, for he and his cousins have swarmed along the Thames of late years. They find food there, and kind people enjoy feeding the screaming birds as they wheel in graceful flight over the bridges and Embankment.

The country boy, too, sees this Gull. He flies far inland, following the plough, and he then rids the land of many a harmful grub. Because of this habit, some people call him the Sea-crow. At all seaside places you find him, and there he fights for his meals with the Herring Gull, the Common Gull, the Kittiwake and others.

Really we should call this gull the Brown-headed, not the Black-headed, Gull; for the hood is more brown than black; and again, if you look for this bird during your summer holidays, you will see no dark hood on his head. You might, though, know him then by the red legs and bill, and the white front-edging to his lovely pearly-grey wings.

Look at him in January, however, and you see dark feathers beginning to appear on his head. The fact is, this dark hood is the bird's wedding dress. It comes only when the nesting season draws near. Then he leaves the fields, parks, and rivers, to fly away to the nesting-place.

These Gulls love to nest in colonies--that is, near one another. Among rushes and reeds, and rough grass growing in deep wet mud, they feel that their nests are safe. There they lay three eggs. The chicks, almost as soon as they leave the eggs, can run about. If there is no dry land near the nest, these youngsters tumble in the water and swim without bothering about swimming lessons.

In summer they are ready to fly with their parents round the coast, and to the muddy mouths of large rivers, where they feed. Flocks of them are also seen out in the open sea, feeding on the shoals of small fish. They also follow steamers, for the sake of any scraps thrown overboard, and they crowd round the fishing boats when they are being unloaded. You see, they are *scavengers*, and so are to be found wherever there are waste scraps of food.

Perhaps you have noticed that Gulls float high in the sea, like so many corks. They can leave the water easily, and take to flight; but they *cannot* dive. The Gull's dinner-table is the whole coast. His eyes are keen enough, as you will know if you have watched him swoop down on a piece of bread in mid-air, and catch it neatly in his beak.

The flight of this Gull is beautiful, graceful, and easy. Sometimes he wheels up and up into the blue sky, almost without moving a wing. He can also glide for a great while, balancing his body against the wind, and turning his head from side to side on the look-out for food. Those long, pointed wings of his make him one of Nature's most perfect flying-machines. His wild, laughing cry has given him the nickname of Laughing Gull.

In the fields and along the banks of our big rivers you may see the Common Gull with numbers of his black-headed cousins. His beak and legs and webbed feet are greenish yellow, and this is quite enough to distinguish the two birds. Their habits are much the same. Both skim over the sea, or the coast, looking for waste food. They are not very "choice" in their meals; dead fish or live fish, young crabs, worms, shell-fish or grubs they eat readily, as well as any offal thrown from passing ships, or the refuse of the fish-market.

One of these scavenging birds was seen to be carrying a long object, like an eel, in its mouth. The bird was shot; and it was then discovered that the "eel" was really a string of candles! The greedy Gull had half-swallowed one, leaving the rest to hang down from its bill. The Common Gull nests in "colonies," like the Black-headed Gull. Its nest is made of seaweed, heather, and dried grass, in which it lays its three greenish-brown eggs.

Another bird to be seen along all parts of our coast, summer and winter alike, is the Cormorant, usually with a small party of his friends. They fly swiftly, one behind the other, and a long line of them reminds one of the pictures of "sea-serpents," especially as they fly quite near the surface of the sea, each one with its long neck outstretched. The Gull flies beautifully, as if he knew his power, and loved to show how he can skim and dive through the air. The Cormorant is not a flier, but a swimmer and diver; he cannot "show off" in the air, and only uses his narrow wings to take him, as quickly as may be, from one fishing-place to another.

Most of the Cormorant's time is spent in fishing, for he lives entirely on fish, and catches immense numbers of them. He spends many hours, too, in drying his wings. I once saw a number of these birds with their wings "hung out to dry." Each one was perched on a stump of wood, across the muddy mouth of a river, and each sooty-looking bird had his wings wide open in the sun. This habit seems to show that the Cormorant uses his wings, as well as his feet, in his frequent journeys under water.

The powerful webbed feet of the Cormorant, set far back on the body, the darting head, long neck, and long curved beak, tell you plainly how he earns his meals. He is a clever fish-hunter, and the fishermen, knowing the appetite of this keen rival of theirs, detest him and destroy him. In some countries there is a price on his head--that is, so much money is given for every Cormorant killed.

Sometimes the Cormorant swims slowly along with his head under water, on the watch for small fish. Seeing one below him, he dives like a flash, and can remain under water for some time; he wastes very little time, however, in swallowing his victim head first.

The great skill of this bird has been made use of, and tame Cormorants are used in China to obtain fish for their masters. They have been used in England, too, for the same purpose. A strap is placed round the bird's neck to prevent him from swallowing the catch. He is then set to work. After catching five or six fish he is recalled by his master, and made to disgorge his prey, which, of course, he has swallowed as far as the strap will permit.

The Cormorant is famous for his large appetite; he chases even big fish, of a size to choke him, you would think. Like his relative the Pelican, he owns a very elastic throat. I have seen a Pelican put a half-grown duck in its pouch, without much trouble. The Cormorant could not perform this feat, but his throat will stretch so as to allow the passage of large fish. Small fish he usually tosses up in the air, catches them neatly head first, and swallows them whole.

Another bird of our coast is the Oyster-catcher, sometimes called the "Sea-pie" or Mussel-picker. These names suit it well, for it does not live on oysters, but on mussels, limpets and whelks. Of course, these are easily "caught" at low tide; they are not easily eaten, so the Sea-pie has to earn his dinner by hard work. In fact, his beak is often notched by the sharp, hard edges of the shells of these molluscs; and at times, he haunts the low banks of mud and ooze near the sea, and there picks up worms and other soft-bodied animals.

As his name Sea-pie shows, the Oyster-catcher is a black-and-white bird, his under parts being white and upper parts black. His legs and long, straight bill are red. Most birds of the waterside seem to find that black-and-white feathers make a good disguise. Though they would show up plainly on a green field, they are well hidden among the stones along the edge of the water.

The Sea-pie makes no nest, only a hole in the sand or shingle, lined with small stones or shells. The eggs are coloured and marked so that they are hard to see among the stones which surround them. The youngsters wear a fluffy suit of grey, marked with dark streaks and dots; and it takes very sharp eyes indeed to pick them out from the shingle where they crouch.

The Ringed Plover is another bird which loves the sandy, pebbly margin of the sea. Have you ever watched him there? He is not much larger than a plump lark, and he runs quickly along the beach, stooping now and again to pick up the morsels of food which his keen eye detects.

But, all the while, he is watching you with the other eye, for he is a wary little bird, and not to be taken by surprise. *If* you can get near him, you will notice his rather long yellowish legs, greyish-brown back, and, more than all, the white collar round his neck, and the black band showing on his white chest. Again we see the black-and-white markings which are so useful to the bird of the shore.

Everyone who knows the Ringed Plover loves to watch him. He is one of the daintiest, most fairy-like birds. When he is picking up worms and sand-hoppers on the wet sand he is easily observed. But wait! He flies off and settles on the shingle not far away. You walk nearer, to watch him. Alas! he is gone. You know just where he settled, yet he is gone! He has often played that trick on me.

The secret lies in his grey, white-and-black markings. When our ships were in danger from enemy submarines, our sailors painted them with queer stripes and bars, to make it hard for the enemy to see them. Nature has marked the Ringed Plover on the same plan. The feathers are so coloured and the colours are so arranged that, once among the grey, yellow, black, and white pebbles on the beach, the little bird is invisible. It is as if the earth had swallowed him up.

The eggs, too, are just as hard to find. There is no nest to "give the game away"; and the eggs look just like the pebbles amongst which they are laid. The young ones are protected from their enemies in the same way, and they crouch, as still as death, amid the stones which they so much resemble.

Now let us leave the beach and look for the Redshank on the mud-flats. Many birds would starve there, but the Redshank is quite happy, as Nature has fitted him for his life in such a place. His long, red legs--from which he gets his name--are for wading in the shallow, muddy creeks he loves. Those wide-spreading feet keep him from sinking in the mud.

The long beak is for probing. As a rule the Redshank digs for his dinner, though he also picks up any worms or other food on the surface; but he is nearly always seen probing the mud.

Like all the shore birds, Redshanks are very wary. They have no hedges or trees for hiding-places, and so must always be on the watch. No sooner does the Redshank spy you than he is up and, with a shrill whistle of alarm, flies quickly away.

The marshes are the home of many a bird like the Redshank. They are all waders and diggers. They live much as he does, and so they have the long beak and legs, and the spreading feet, to fit them for that life.

We have now looked at a few sea birds, shore birds, and a marsh bird. Many inland birds, too, are fond of the shore. The artful Jackdaw builds in the cliffs, and his cousin, the Crow, searches the shore for food. Even the gay Kingfisher has been seen diving in the seaside pools.

THE REDSHANK.

EXERCISES

1. How do you know which is the Black-headed Gull in the summer months?

2. Why is it difficult to see the Ringed Plover on the stones of the shore?

3. Where would you look for the eggs of the Ringed Plover and of the Black-headed Gull?

4. Why have marsh birds such long beaks?

LESSON IV.

CRABS.

Little Crabs are to be found everywhere along the sea-shore--not the monsters of the fishmonger's shop, but small greenish-brownish Crabs. They live in the weed of the rock-pools, and in the wet sand. These are the Shore Crabs; the large Edible Crabs are a different kind, and live mostly in deep water.

Shore Crabs are quarrelsome little creatures; the larger ones are always ready to gobble up the smaller ones, or to snatch their food and run away with it. If you put some dead mussels or fish in a pool, you will be amused at their antics. How they scramble and fight! Crabs do not believe in "table manners."

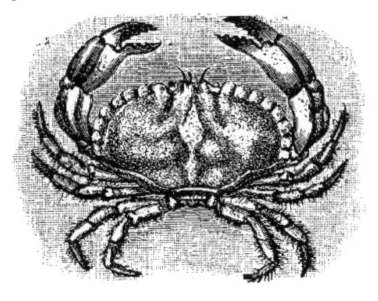

THE CRAB.

It is their taste for waste scraps of food that makes crabs of use in the sea. They are most useful scavengers. They clear the sea and beach of dead matter which would poison the air and water.

For many years nobody knew how Crabs grew up. It was thought that a baby Crab was like its mother, just as a baby spider is a tiny picture of its parent. But no, the young Crab is as much *like* a Crab as a caterpillar is like a butterfly.

Let us begin at the beginning--the egg. Mother Crab carries her eggs with her, under her tail, which itself is always kept tucked up under her body. Out of each egg there comes the queerest little creature! It is just large enough to be seen as it wriggles in the water. Then its skin splits, and there appears a quaint thing with long feathery legs, a big head, a spike on the back of its head, and another spike like a nose.

Who would suspect this strange atom would turn into a Crab! Well, nobody did. It was called a *zoea*; but you can call it a Crab caterpillar or larva. The maggot is the larva of the fly, and the zoea is the larva of the Crab. With crowds of its brothers and sisters, the zoea kicks about on the surface of the sea. Fishes, and even great whales, swallow these tiny things by the million.

The Crab larva eats and grows. Again and again its skin splits, and a rather different zoea appears. This happens about once a week, until, hey presto! the spiked zoea is now rather like a Crab. The spikes are gone, and now it has tiny claws, and two eyes at the end of stalks. Yet it still owns a tail. At last this is tucked up under its body, and lo! our little friend has changed into a very small Crab. No longer able to swim about, it comes to get a living in the shallow pools of the shore.

Luckily, this helpless baby knows how to hide. He is helped by his colour, for it matches the green and brown of the weeds and rocks. He knows how to dig himself into the sand, and work his shell well down. Then only his funny eyes on stalks peer up at you. At this time of his life he has to "make himself scarce," and snatch his food when and where he can.

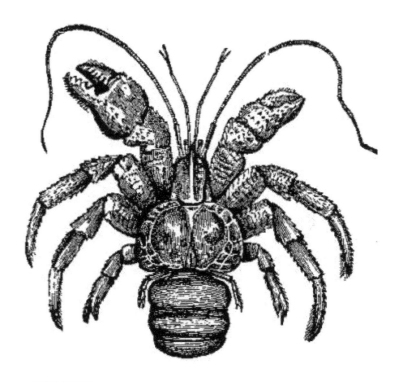

PURSE CRAB.

We do not eat these little Crabs, but other Crabs do, and so do anemones, gulls, and other hungry creatures; and they themselves hunt sand-hoppers, and eat anything they can find or steal. So they grow bigger; and then, like the boy who grows quickly, the Crab finds his shelly suit a size too small for him!

Now look at his suit. It is a hard coat, a complete suit of armour to protect his soft body. Our picture shows the Lobster, the Crab's cousin. The Shrimp and Prawn and Lobster are relations of the Crab; these *crustaceans*, as they are called, are all cased up in a hard *crust*, which will not stretch the slightest little bit. But the Crab's body *must* grow! What is he to do?

At first he starves himself, and so his body shrinks inside its old shell. He loosens himself as well as he can. Soon the shell breaks across, and the Crab struggles to get free. At last he backs out, and leaves his old suit for ever. It is a wonderful performance, for he has withdrawn even from the legs, claws, feelers, bristles, eye-stalks and eyes! The old shell is left quite whole--a perfect Crab, but with no Crab inside it!

Now the Crab, in his new suit, hides away. He knows that he is a soft, flabby creature at this time, and that other animals, even Mrs. Crab, would be glad to meet him--and eat him. While his covering is yet soft he grows quickly. When it is hard, he ventures out again, ready to quarrel and fight.

This change of shell happens often to young Crabs. Older ones change only once a year. All the different kinds of Crab begin life as *larvae* or *zoeas*, and cast their shells as we have seen.

Crabs can see and hear and smell; and they must also have a fine sense of touch. I was once watching a big Crab eating his dinner under a rocky ledge in a large glass tank. As he tore his food, some of the bits, no larger than crumbs, fell and settled on the rocks below. Then I saw that a smaller Crab, with long pincers, was hiding under a rock. As the crumbs fell, he reached out his pincers and picked them up, one by one. Each bit was gravely carried to his mouth, and tucked in, and then he reached out for another. Though I was very close to the Crab, I could hardly see the tiny scraps which he was able to pick up so easily.

One of the strangest Crabs is the Hermit. You would think that Nature had played a joke on him, for he has only half a suit of armour. His tail part is soft. He would have a bad time in the sea, but for a dodge he has learnt.

The baby Hermit takes the empty home of a periwinkle. As he grows he needs a larger house, and so leaves the tight shell and pops his tail into a bigger one, generally a whelk shell. If he meets with another Hermit there is a battle, one trying to steal the other's shell. Our coloured picture, page 35, shows some Hermits at war. Fighting, house-hunting, and moving house seem to be the Hermit's favourite pursuits. But, whatever he does, his first care is to protect that soft tail of his. His right claw is large and strong, so he uses it to close the door of his stolen home.

Sometimes he has a lodger who lives on the roof. This lodger, as you will notice in our coloured picture, is the sea anemone. The Hermit and his lodger seem to be good friends, at least they seem to like each other's company. There is no doubt that there are good reasons for this. We shall have more to say about this strange pair in our lesson on the sea anemones.

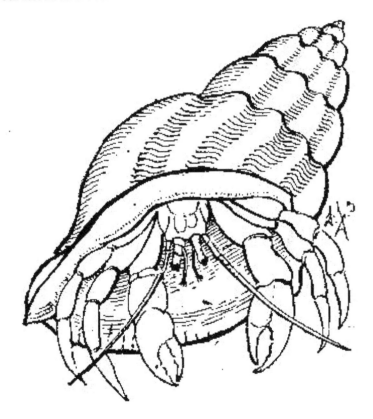

HERMIT CRAB IN WHELK'S SHELL.

Another funny Crab is the Spider Crab. Its back is covered with reddish bristles, like so many hooks. These catch in the seaweed, and soon the Spider Crab is decorated with bits of weed. But that is not all. The artful Crab tears off other pieces of weed with its pincers, and attaches them to the hooks. It is another dodge, of course, to escape from enemies. The Lobster, whose picture you see, has a life-story much like that of the Crab. He, also, grows too big for his suit of armour, and casts it off in a wonderful manner, but only after a great deal of trouble. In his new suit he is very weak and soft--an easy prey to the first enemy to find him. He cannot defend himself then; he can only lie helplessly on his side, waiting for his coat to harden. He is so weak that his soft legs cannot bear the weight of his body.

HERMIT CRABS FIGHTING.

Needless to say, the Lobster always finds a secure retreat before casting off his protecting coat of armour. A hole under a rock suits him well at that time. Strange to say, he seems to dislike his old clothes, and often crunches them to pieces or eats them up, or even pushes them under the sand or stones! Then he marches out like a proud warrior, knowing his strength, and the power of his great claws.

Lobsters are fond of fighting, and must be very disagreeable neighbours. They can swim along by using the little "swimmerets" under their bodies. Or, by rapidly bending down their powerful tails, Lobsters are able to shoot backwards through the water at a great pace. In our next lesson we shall find that Prawns are also able to paddle forwards or dart backwards in a similar way.

Lobsters, living and dead, are often on sale in the fishmonger's shop. Like the Crabs and Prawns, they are usually caught in traps or pots, baited with pieces of fish, and left among the rocks. The traps are of various shapes, some being like bee-hives made of cane or wicker; others are made of netting stretched over hoops, and more like a bird-cage in shape.

The Lobster smells the bait in the trap, and hastens to get to it by diving through the only entrance. Having enjoyed his meal he tries to swim away; but there is no escape, and there he must wait until the owner of the trap makes his usual "round" in the morning. Of course, there is a rope to every trap, and a cork to mark its position.

HERMIT CRAB WITH SEA FLOWERS.

Then the Lobster finds himself taken carefully out of prison; his claws are tied to prevent him from fighting, and he goes to market with a lot of other Lobsters. There are many lobster fisheries along the rocky parts of our coast.

HERMIT CRAB WITH SEA FLOWERS.

You will often see Lobsters with one very large claw, and one small. They are able to throw off a limb or two whenever they are frightened. Also they often lose a claw in the terrible fights of which they seem so fond. If one joint of a claw becomes injured the Lobster has no further use for it; he is wise, for his very life depends on his armour. So he throws it away, not at the wounded joint, but at the joint above.

After a time a slight swelling appears on the stump thus made; this gradually grows into a new limb. It may be smaller than the lost one, but it is perfect in detail. What a useful gift this must be to an animal like the Lobster, whose whole life is one terrible fight after another!

The baby Lobsters, like the baby Crabs, are quite unlike their parents. They swim about at the surface of the sea, and already they seize every chance of fighting and eating their small neighbours.

When about one inch in length they leave this infants' school, and join another at the bottom of the sea. Here they eat, fight, grow and change their coats, just as the young Crabs do. They are now like their parents. Sometimes they grow to be huge, and to weigh as much as ten-and-a-half pounds.

The mother Lobster carries as many as thirty thousand eggs under her body! Needless to say, a very, very few of this enormous family survive the dangers of the sea. The rule there is--"Eat and be eaten!".

THE LOBSTER.

EXERCISES

1. What is a Crab larva like?

2. Give the names of four crustaceans.

3. Why does the Crab have to change its shell?

4. Why does it hide away at that time?

5. Of what use are Shore Crabs?

6. How are Lobsters caught?

LESSON V.

SHRIMPS, PRAWNS AND BARNACLES.

In nearly every shore-pool you may see Shrimps and Prawns darting out of sight, and, for every one you see, there are many more hidden away. These delicate, transparent, lively creatures are not much like the boiled Shrimps and Prawns of the fish-shop.

They are the prey of so many fish, crabs, and birds, that they have learnt to "make themselves scarce." Have you ever watched them in a glass tank, or aquarium? If so, you will know that it is not easy to see them. In the shore-pools it is harder still.

Some are swaying about in the still, clear water, moving their long feelers from side to side. Others have burrowed into the sand. In doing this, they raise a sandy cloud, which settles on them and hides them. To catch some, you must use a "shrimp-net," for they can dart across the pool like arrows.

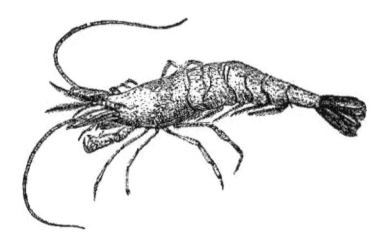

THE SHRIMP.

Some are Shrimps, and some are Prawns; how can we tell the difference? When they are boiled the answer is easy. All the Shrimps turn brown and the Prawns red. (The red "Shrimps" are near relations of the Prawn.) To tell a live Shrimp from a Prawn, look at the long pointed beak which juts out from the front of the head. That of the Prawn is toothed, like a little saw. If the beak is quite smooth its wearer is a Shrimp.

Until Prawns are grown up, they haunt the sandy shallows with their cousins the Shrimps. But the larger Prawns live in deeper water. They are generally caught in traps, as are their relatives, the crab and lobster.

Now look closely at a Prawn, and try to find how it swims. Turn it upside down. It has ten legs; and, under each of the horny rings of its body, you can see a pair of little paddles. They are fringed with hairs. When the Prawn or Shrimp is not in a hurry, he swims slowly but surely with the little paddles, or "swimmerets." If any danger threatens, he uses his tail, in this way:--It is made of five fringed plates, which, as you can see, spread out or close up, like a fan. As he doubles up his body, the plates spread themselves out. They strike the water with great force, and so send the Prawn or Shrimp quickly *backwards*. As the body becomes straight again, the fan closes, ready for another stroke. To move quickly, the Shrimp or Prawn merely bends his body, then straightens it. The tail thus becomes a strong oar, driving him backwards with rapid jerks.

Look now at the Prawn's long, hair-like feelers. There are two pairs. On one pair are the ears, a special kind of ear for hearing in water.

You will notice that the Shrimp's eyes are on the end of short stalks. Each big eye is really a cluster of little eyes, rather like the "compound eyes" of insects. If you lift up the horny shield behind the head, you see a row of what look like curly feathers. These are the breathing gills.

Shrimps carry their eggs about with them; no doubt you have often found masses of eggs under the Shrimp's body. Each egg is fastened by a kind of "glue," or else the rapid jerking of the mother Shrimp would soon loosen the eggs and set them free.

The hard, shelly covering of the Shrimp and Prawn is like the armour of the crab--it will not stretch in the least. The body is easily bent, owing to the soft hinges between the hard rings. But the coat itself will not stretch. Then how do these little creatures grow? We see small Shrimps and large ones, so grow they must, in some way.

They are of the same family--the *crustacea*--as the crab; and they grow in much the same way. The hard covering gets too tight for the body inside it. Then it splits across the back. After much wriggling, the Shrimp appears in a new soft skin. While the skin is still soft the Shrimp grows very quickly. Crustaceans have a funny way of growing, have they not? Instead of growing evenly, little by little, they grow by "fits and starts," a great deal in a few hours and then not at all.

Besides being good food for us, and for the fish, Shrimps and Prawns have another use. They are scavengers. They pick to pieces and eat the vegetable and animal stuff which floats in the sea. Before it can decay and become poisonous, these useful creatures use it up as food. Great numbers of Shrimps and Prawns are caught for our markets. Some are caught by men who push a small net over the sands near shore, but most are caught by the *shrimp-trawl*, a large net cast from a small sailing vessel.

The rocks, and the wooden piles of the pier, are often covered with the hard shells known as Barnacles, or Acorn Shells. If you slip on them with bare feet their sharp edges cut you. Each Acorn Shell is a little house. Have you ever caught a glimpse of the animal living inside?

If you will look very carefully, you will see that the Acorn Shell is made of three-sided pieces, closely joined. There is a little door at the top, kept tightly closed until the tide comes up and covers the rocks. Then watch, and you will see a bunch of tiny feathers appear through a slit in the door. This means that the animal is hungry, and has put its twelve legs out of doors to catch a dinner!

This is strange, but true! The Barnacle is always upside down in its home, and its twelve feathery legs are thrust out of the door at the top. They make a fine net, in which minute animals are caught and brought into the mouth below. This funny creature actually kicks its food into its mouth! If you own a magnifying glass, you can see this for yourself at the seaside.

You will not be able to see the mouth, however, which is inside the shell. It is fitted with moving parts, and feelers, like the mouth of a crab. Also, the Barnacle has a good set of teeth to grind its food. It has no real eyes, having no use for them. Of what use are eyes to an animal standing on its head in a small dark shell! Now and then it casts its coat (like the Crab and Shrimp). The old coat is rolled up and thrown away outside the door.

Now comes the strangest thing of all. As a baby, the Barnacle is a free swimming creature. It has three pairs of legs, a tail, a useful mouth, and one eye. After kicking about in the sea for some time, and changing its skin, it changes its shape entirely. It now looks more like a tiny mussel. It has two little "shells," two eyes, legs, and feelers. Now its swimming days are nearly over, and it must settle down. It gives up eating, and roves about looking and feeling for a place to settle on.

Finding a suitable spot, the little animal stands on its head. Then a kind of glue is formed, which fixes it for life to that place, head down. The two shells and the two eyes are now thrown off. The Barnacle quickly builds up a shelly house, and, after a life of adventure and change, becomes a fixed Barnacle for the rest of its days.

For many years people knew little of this strange animal. All its wonderful changes, and the way its body is made, tell us plainly that the Barnacle is actually first cousin to the Crab, Lobster, Shrimp and Prawn! It belongs to the class known as the *Crustacea*; but, for some reason or other, it has chosen to live its grown-up life fixed to a rock.

EXERCISES

1. How does the Shrimp swim?

2. Of what use are Shrimps and Prawns in the sea?

3. How can you tell a live Shrimp from a live Prawn?

4. How does the Barnacle obtain its food?

5. Give the names of five crustaceans.

LESSON VI.

PLANTS OF THE SHORE.

To pick a bunch of gay flowers you would look in the fields and hedge-rows, and not by the sea. Flowers, as you know, love moist soil, and not dry sand; and, like us, they prefer one food to another. Sand they do not like, and salt is a poison to them. Both of these are enemies to plant life.

Also, flowers choose sheltered spots. They do not like rough winds, and the glare of the sun shrivels them up. Yet there are plants with pretty flowers to be found by the sea, and many others with small, dull flowers. These seaside plants have to fight for their lives. The dry, shifting sand, and the salt spray, are enough to kill them, you would think. They have no shelter from the strong sea wind, nor from the fierce glare of the summer sun. The puzzle is, how do they live among so many enemies? For you know that the flowers of the field would at once die if you planted them in salt and sand. They would starve to death.

Even the strongest seaside plants shun that part of the beach washed by the waves. They leave that to the seaweeds.

Let us look first at some plants which have their home on the sand-hills. Here is a fine one, like a thistle, with stiff prickly leaves, and a stiff blue stem. In August it has blue-grey flowers. This plant is called Sea Holly, its leaves being like those of the holly. It has an unpleasant smell, yet its roots are used for making some kinds of sweets.

Now try to pull up a plant of Sea Holly. You find it no easy task. Then dig away the sand, and you see that its large roots have gone deep and far. All these plants of sandy places grow like that. Sand has no food or drink to give to plants. So they send their roots out, like plants in a desert, until they find what they want. Besides food and drink, they need a firm anchor in the loose sand. The Sea Holly, with its roots deep down and far-spreading, can hold its own, though the gale tears at it and throws its sandy bed here and there.

We pass many small creeping plants as we walk in the dry sand. There is a pretty Sea Convolvulus, with its stems deeply buried. It is a cousin of the common Bindweed. Then we see many plants of Thyme, and a few ragged bushes of Gorse. We notice that several little plants grow near the Gorse, as if they had crept there for shelter. The sea breeze has blown the sand into heaps, and even on these dry, thirsty hillocks we see many tufts of grass.

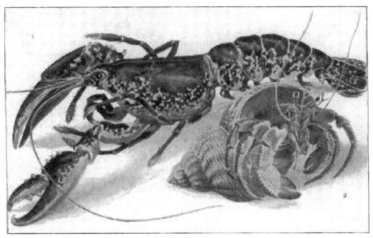

1. THE COMMON LOBSTER.   2. HERMIT CRAB.

These Couch Grasses and Dune Grasses, as they are often called, are coarse and hard. Cattle pass them by in disgust. Yet they are the most useful plants on the shore. They can live and spread where other plants die. They have very long underground stems, which go through and through the dry, loose sand. The wind does its best to bury them in sand, but they send up hard, sharp buds, and go on living, and spreading.

Bit by bit, the sand is held together by the matted stems of these grasses. It becomes firm, instead of loose; the wind can no longer blow it about. Then other plants can grow in that place. You know how men go out to the wild parts of the earth and, by hard work, make those places ready for others to settle there. Well, the sand-grass works like that. It prepares the way for useful plants to grow in places where they could not grow before.

Quite near to the sea we shall find a very strange little plant. It has no leaves, only fleshy, jointed stems. It is known as the Glass-wort, being full of a substance useful in making glass. It belongs to a family which seems to delight in deserts and salty soil! They have all sorts of dodges to help them live in such places. For instance, their leaves are fleshy. Squeeze them, and they are like wet, juicy fruit.

The Sea Beet is also a member of this family. The Red Beet, as well as the Mangel-wurzel, we owe to this humble seaside plant. Most of our sugar comes from the Sugar-beet.

Another useful plant is the Sea Cabbage, which grows on some parts of our sea coast. It is rather a ragged, tough kind of Cabbage, and perhaps you would not choose it for your dinner-table. We have more tempting sorts in our gardens--Brussels Sprouts, Brocco-li, Cauliflower, but long, long ago the wild seaside cabbage was the only one growing. Men found it to be eatable, and began to plant it near their huts or caves. From that small beginning all our garden cabbages have come.

Walking a little farther from the sea, we leave the sand and come to stones, rocks and cliffs. We pass a pretty plant, the Sea Lavender, and another, the Sea Stock. They love best the sandy, muddy parts of the shore. Their lilac flowers look bright and pretty. Coming to the rocky places, we find tufts of the flower known as Sea Pink or Thrift. Its leaves are like grass, and its flowers form a round pink bundle at the top of a bare stalk.

There are many tufts of Thrift growing among the rocks; and each tuft has a number of pink flowers. In some places you could step from one tuft to another for several miles. Bare and ugly stretches of coast are made into a gay garden by this lovely flower.

Here and there on the rocks is a plant with large yellow blossoms--the Yellow Horned Poppy. It is a handsome plant, and you are surprised to see such fine flowers among dry shingle, sand, or rock; but the Horned Poppy is well able to stand the salt spray and storms of its favourite home. When the petals have dropped, a green seed-pod is left. It is very long--nearly twice as long as this page and looks much more like a stem than a seed-pod.

Sometimes this seaside poppy is seen growing high up the face of the cliff, where only the jackdaw and sea-birds can find a footing; and many another plant may be seen there too. The cliffs are full of cracks, some tiny and some wide. In these places there is always a certain amount of dirt and grit. You could hardly call it "soil," and most plants would starve if you planted them in such a place.

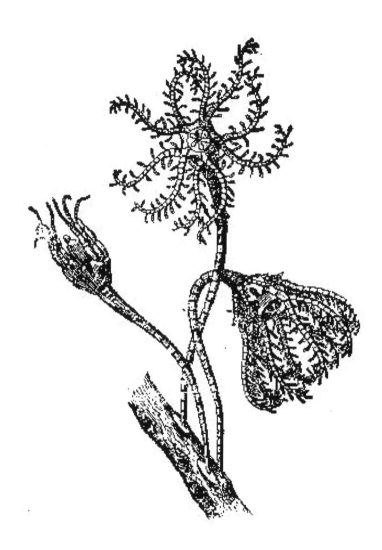

SEA LILY.

These plants of the rock and cliff are not so proud. They have very long and very thin roots, admirably suited to pierce the grit, and explore the cracks in the rock, to find the moisture they need. Besides this, they have fleshy leaves which help them to keep alive. The Stone-crop and the Penny-wort are well-known plants of this kind. They grow where you would least expect to find a living plant. Neither heat nor thirst seems to kill them. Mother Nature has found many a wonderful way of helping her children to live.

EXERCISES

1. Why do plants which grow in sand have such long roots?

2. In what way are the grasses growing on the sand so useful?

3. Give the names of four flowering plants of the shore.

4. Where would you look for the Stone-crop and Penny-wort?

5. Why do these two plants have such thin roots?

LESSON VII.

FLOWER-LIKE ANIMALS.

The prettiest of the creatures of the shore is the Sea Anemone. No one can see it without being reminded of a flower, an Aster or Daisy, with a thick stalk and many coloured petals; but, knowing how it is made, and how it lives, we place it in the Animal Kingdom, though among the lowliest members of that Kingdom. It is a cousin of that strange creature, the Jelly-fish, which we shall look at in another lesson.

SEA ANEMONE.

When the tide falls, you can walk among the rocks and pools by the sea, and find Anemones in plenty. They are fixed to the rocks. Some are under the ledges, out of sight, others are low down, half buried in the wet sand; and others are on the sides of the rocks, looking like blobs of green, brown, or red jelly. Feel one of them. It is slimy, and rather firm, not so soft and yielding as the Jelly-fish. You cannot easily pull it from the rocks without harming it; but you will find other Anemones on stones and shells; and these you can put in a jar of sea-water, with some weed, and carry home to examine later on.

When covered with sea-water the ugly blobs of jelly open out like beautiful flowers. In some places along our coast the floor of the sea is like a flower garden, gay with thousands of coloured Anemones.

Those little "petals" are really *tentacles*, used for catching and holding food. We will use a shorter word and call them feelers. They are set in circles round the top of the Anemone, and there are many of them. The Daisy Anemone, for instance, has over seven hundred feelers. Each feeler can be moved from side to side, and can also be tucked away, out of sight and out of danger; but, when hungry, the animal spreads them widely, for, as we shall see, they are the net in which it catches its dinner.

The whole body of the Anemone is like two bags, one hanging inside the other. The space between the two bags is filled with water. The feelers are hollow tubes which open out of this space; so they, too, are filled with water.

CRUSTACEA.

1. THE LARVA OF A LEAF-BODIED CRUSTACEAN CALLED PHYLLOSOMA.

2. A PRAWN-LIKE CREATURE, SHOWING THE FRONT LIMBS THAT ARE USED FOR GRASPING PREY.

3. A CRAB.

4. THIS IS A SHRIMP-LIKE CREATURE CALLED CUMA SCOR-PIOIDES.

The Anemone can press the water into them, and so force them to open out. In rather the same way you can expand the fingers of a glove by forcing your breath into them. The Anemone, you see, can open or close just as it pleases.

What does it eat, and how does it find food? Perhaps you have watched an open Anemone in a pool, or in a glass tank, and seen it at its meals. A small creature swims near, and touches one of the feelers. Instead of darting away, it appears to be held still; and then other feelers bend towards it and hold the victim. Then they are all drawn to the centre of the Anemone, carrying their prey with them; and the feelers, prey and all, are tucked out of sight.

That is the way the Anemone obtains its food. As soon as the feelers get hold of a small animal they carry it to the opening of a tube in the centre. This is the mouth, leading to the stomach. Very often the feelers, with their victim, are tucked away into the stomach, and the feelers do not appear again for some time. Is not this a strange way of eating!

Much stranger still is the way in which the food is held, and made so helpless that it cannot escape. On the skin of the Anemone there are many thousands of very tiny pockets, or cells. Each cell contains a fine thread with a poisoned barb at the tip, The thread is packed away in the cell, coiled up like the spring of a watch. As soon as anything presses against the cells they shoot out their threads. Thus the tips of many poisoned threads enter the skin of any soft animal which is unlucky enough to touch an Anemone.

If your own skin is tender, these little stinging hairs will irritate it, but not enough to hurt you. It is different, however, with the small creatures of the sea. They are made quite helpless when caught by hundreds of these strange threads. We shall find similar poison-threads in the Jelly-fish; and these, in some cases, can cause us serious illness. You cannot see them without the aid of a microscope.

All those parts of its food which the Anemone cannot digest, it throws out again. If you feed an Anemone on raw meat, it tucks the pieces into its mouth, and, some days after, throws out the hard part of the meat, having taken all the "goodness" from it.

No doubt the Anemones themselves are eaten by other animals in the sea, but many kinds of fish will not touch them. You may remember that we noticed an Anemone which lived on the stolen home of the Hermit Crab. The crab lives in the whelk shell, and the Anemone lives on the roof, as it were. In nearly every ocean, all over the world, these two partners are found, using the same shell. It is thought that the Anemone lives there for two good reasons. First, the Hermit moves from place to place; you can see that this would give the Anemone a better chance of obtaining food. Also, bits of food float to the Anemone when the crab is picking his dinner to pieces.

The crab seems to like having his strange partner with him. No doubt the Anemone is of some use to him, or he would at once pull it off. It is thought that the Anemone protects him from his enemies, the fish. Some of them would swallow the whelk shell, crab and all, but they would not eat one on which an Anemone was fixed. We are not *sure* that these reasons are the right ones. All we know for certain is, that a crab and an Anemone have, for some good reasons, gone into partnership.

Anemones have large families. Sometimes they have numbers of eggs; at other times their little ones come straight into the world as very tiny Anemones. A boy who kept a large Anemone in a tank of sea water, was astonished to find that in a short time, he had not one, but hundreds, of the creatures. The tiny Anemones were fixed to the glass and rock, all fishing for food with their little outspread tentacles. Sometimes the Anemone will calmly divide itself into two, each half becoming a perfect Anemone!

Anemones are of many shapes, sizes, and colours. The loveliest of our British ones is the Plumose Anemone. It is like a carnation, and may grow to be six inches high--that is, nearly as long as this page. It is known by its shape, not by its colour. It may be any of these colours--brown, deep green, pale orange, flesh colour, cream, bright red, brick colour, lemon, or pure white.

There are many other creatures in the sea which resemble plants and are often mistaken for them. The Sea Lily (p.49) is one of the flower-like animals; it is a relative of the Starfish, living in deep water. The Sea Mat (p.59) is often found on the shore. It seems like a horny kind of weed, but is really a colony of tiny animals, each one having its own little cell to live in.

EXERCISES

1. How does the Anemone expand its "feelers"?

2. In what way does the Anemone catch the small animals on which it feeds?

3. Where is the mouth of the Anemone?

4. In what way might the Anemone be of use to its partner, the hermit crab?

LESSON VIII.

SEA-WEEDS AND SEA-GRASS

We think of weeds as useless plants which insist on growing just where they are not wanted. So it is a pity that *Sea-weeds* are so named, for the part they play in the sea is a useful one; and they are often beautiful, though they do not bear flowers like so many plants of the land. You see draggled heaps of them, lying on the shore where the waves have thrown them. They are best seen in their proper home, buoyed up by the water, and spreading out their broad coloured fronds, or long waving threads. There are, in many places, meadows of Sea-grass, and forests of Sea-weed! Mother Earth still has her carpet of green, even when covered by the salt water. The plants are very unlike those of the land, but, as you will see, they are of great use. We will suppose you put on a diving dress. Then you can walk out, under the water, and explore the forests of the sea.

Down by the line of low tide, before you have waded up to your knees, you find plants clinging to the rocks. They cover them with a slippery coat of green; when you turn these Sea-weeds over you find periwinkles and other animals feeding or hiding. Sea-weed makes good "cover" for the creatures of the rock-pools, who have many enemies to fear.

You notice that most of these shore weeds are green, sometimes as green as young grass. Pull up a bunch of the weed, and you find that it clings to the rocks and stones, but has no real roots. Seaweeds belong to a humble family in the world of plants, having no real roots, no flowers, and no real seeds. They can attach themselves to the stones or rocks. Along comes a great wave, and perhaps they are torn up; but this does not harm them, for they still live as they wash to and fro in the water, until they cling to another rock. Or they are thrown on the shore to die, or else to be washed back to sea by the next tide.

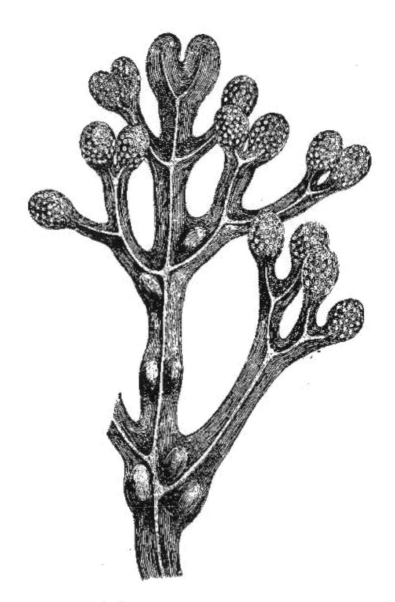

SEA-WEED FROND.

The Sea Lettuce or Green Laver is a common seaweed near the shore. Its broad, crinkled and bright green leaves are rather like those of a lettuce. Sometimes it is boiled to a jelly and used for food. Many other sea-weeds are good to eat, and on some coasts there is a regular sea-weed harvest.

Now wade into rather deeper water, and you find a great mass of the Bladder Wrack. Most schoolboys know it, for the little bladders of air in the leaves explode with a pop if you squeeze them. The Bladder Wrack, and others of the same kind, are torn up by the fierce waves in a storm, and tossed on the beach in heaps. They are gathered by the farmer who knows how to value a cheap manure for his fields. Some kinds are also of use in packing lobsters so that they come to market nice and fresh.

When you have walked--in your diving dress--to deep water, you find yourself among a tangle of olive-green weeds. They are below the line of low tide. All round you is a forest of dark-green ribbons with wavy edges. The ribbons are tough and very long, and cling tightly to the rocks. These ribbon-weeds, and others of the same kind, are known as Tangles. Round some parts of our coast they make wide, thick beds in the sea. Though the ribbons may be six feet long, they are not so wide as the palm of your hand.

Another sea plant, which grows in tufts in rather deep water, is called Irish Moss; it is green, brown or purple in colour. I do not know why it should be called Irish Moss, for it is not a moss, and it grows all round the English, as well as the Irish, sea-coast. But sea-weeds have strange names; indeed, many of them have no everyday names at all. Irish Moss is used for food, after being boiled to a jelly. It can also be made into a gum or glue, and has often been so used.

Now, if you were to walk still farther on the bed of the sea, into deeper water, you would find the prettiest of all the sea plants. These are the pink and red sea-weeds. You also find them on the beach, but only after they have been torn from their home in the deep water. They grow on the rocks, in pretty coloured tufts.

If you dive still farther, into the dark depths of the sea, you find beds of ooze and slime, and rocks and weird fishes, but no plants. Why is this? Like the land-plants, these sea-plants must have *light*. They cannot grow in the blackness of very deep water. Can you guess why some sea-weeds are green and others red? Those growing in the shallow water of the shore are green, like land-plants, because the sunlight reaches them. Only part of the light can pass through deep water; and so, in these shady places, the sea-weed is reddish in colour.

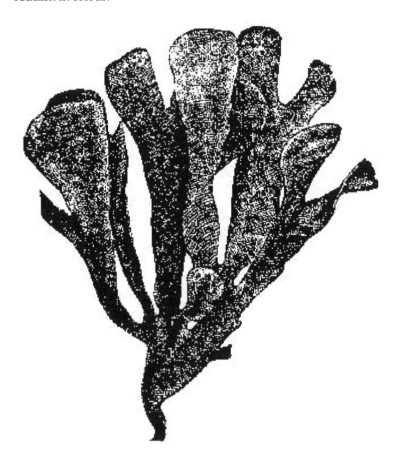

SEA MAT.

We see, then, that (1) green sea-weed grows by the shore; (2) brownish-green sea-weed likes deeper water; (3) red sea-weed grows in deep water; and (4) in very deep water there is no weed at all.

We must not forget the grass of the sea. It grows in narrow blades, often a yard in length, and as wide as your thumb. It is not a sea-weed, but a real flowering plant, which, for some reason or other, loves to grow under water. It creeps in the sand and mud, with green leaves growing up as thick as corn in a cornfield.

All these waving green leaves make large meadows in the sea; and sea-snails, fishes, and crabs hide in it, just as all manner of living things hide in the grass of our meadows. The proper name of this strange plant is Sea Wrack. When dried, it is useful for packing up china, and covering flasks of oil.

Now we come to the real use of sea plants. They are food for all the hosts of small animals of the sea. These eat it as it grows; or else, like the mussel and oyster, swallow the tiny scraps of it which float everywhere like so much dust.

The shell-fish, and other animals which feed on sea plants, are themselves eaten by other sea creatures, and these in their turn are eaten by crabs, lobsters and fish, which are eaten by us. It reminds you of a chain. The first link in the chain is the sea plant, the last links are the fish and ourselves. So, you see, the weeds and grass of the ocean are of very great value indeed.

EXERCISES

1. Give the names of three common Sea-weeds.

2. What is the colour of the weed found in deep water?

3. Why cannot Sea-weed grow in very deep water?

4. In what way are sea plants most useful?

LESSON IX.

THE JELLY-FISH.

Or all the queer children of Nature which live in the sea, the Jelly-fish is one of the queerest. You often find it on the shore, especially after a severe storm. There it lies, a mass of helpless jelly, which slips and breaks through your fingers if you try to lift it.

It cannot move back to its watery home, and in a short time the sun's warmth will have dried it up, leaving but a mark on the sand, and a few scraps of animal matter; for these strange creatures are little else but water. A Jelly-fish, which weighed two pounds when alive, would leave less than the tenth part of one ounce when dried!

There is a story of a farmer who, on seeing thousands and thousands of Jelly-fish along the shore, thought he would make use of them. He decided that they would serve as manure for his fields, and so save him much money. He went home, and sent men with wagons to be loaded with the Jelly-fish. This was done, and the Jelly-fish were spread over the soil. On looking at his fields the next morning, the farmer was astonished to find that every scrap of his new manure had vanished as if by magic!

In the sea the Jelly-fish looks like an umbrella of bluish-white jelly, from which hang tassels and threads. Look over the side of a boat, or from the pier, and you often see them drifting by, hundreds of them, like so many ghosts.

Each one is moving along, with its edges partly opening and shutting. It is plain that this waving motion causes the creatures to move through the water. Also, they can rise to the surface, or fall to the depths, and do not collide with one another. So the Jelly-fish is not at all helpless.

At night Jelly-fishes sometimes look very beautiful. Each one shines in the water, with a soft yet strong light, like fairy lamps afloat in the sea.

They are of all sizes. Some you could put in a small wineglass, others measure nearly two feet across. Evidently the Jelly-fish grows, and, in order to live and grow, it must eat; but what does it eat, and how does it obtain its food?

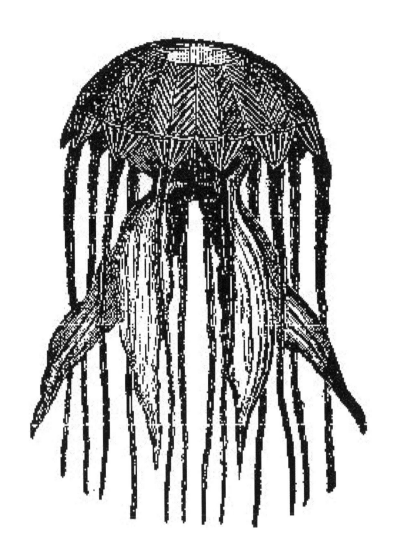

MEDUSA.

Before noticing the wonderful way in which this animal finds its
dinner, let us look at its body. In any large Jelly-fish you can see

marks which run from the centre of the body, and another mark round the edge of the "umbrella." These are really tubes. They all join with a hollow space inside the body, which is the creature's stomach. The mouth-tube opens under the body, as can be seen by turning the Jelly-fish on its back, and moving the lobes of jelly aside. All the food goes up this tube-mouth, and so into the stomach of the animal. The whole creature is little more than so many cells of sea-water, the walls of the cells being a very thin, transparent kind of skin.

Perhaps the strangest thing about it is the way in which it catches prey. Jelly-fish feed on all kinds of tiny sea animals, such as baby fish, and the young of crabs, shrimps, and prawns. These small creatures form part of the usual dinner of many a hungry dweller in the sea, and the Jelly-fish takes a share of them.

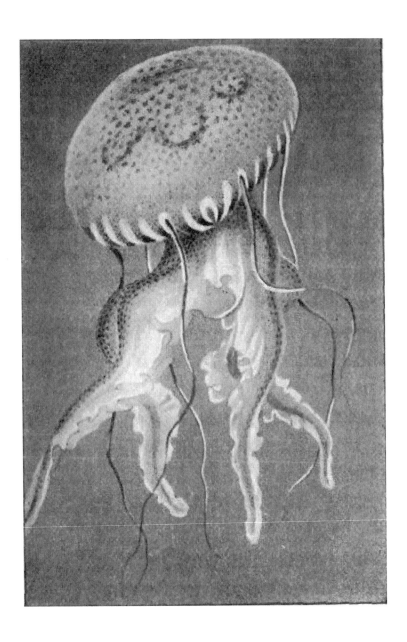

A MEDUSOID.

From the edge of the "umbrella" there hangs a fringe of long, delicate hairs, rather like spiders' threads. These are fishing lines, yet much more deadly. They trail through the water, stretching far from the main part of the Jelly-fish; and any small creature unlucky enough to touch them is doomed.

Down each one of these threads there are minute cells, hundreds and hundreds to every thread; and in each cell there is a dart, coiled up like the spring of a watch. The tip of the dart is barbed like a fishhook. Now the cells are so made that they fly open when touched. The dart then leaps out and buries itself in the skin of the animal which touched the thread. Not only that, but the darts are poisoned, and soon kill the small creatures which they pierce.

You see now how this innocent-looking Jelly-fish gets its food. As it swims along, the threads touch the tiny living things in the sea, the darts pierce them and poison them. Of course these stinging darts are very, very small, much too small for our eyes to see.

Sometimes there are numbers of large brownish Jelly-fish in the sea, or washed up on the shore. If you are paddling or swimming, keep well away from them. Their poison darts are able to pierce through thin skin, and may cause you illness and great pain. Remember that the threads are very long; after you have passed the main body of the animal, you may still be in danger from the trailing threads.

We noticed these same poison darts when we were dealing with the flower-like animals, the Anemones. Only, in that case, they were so fine, so small, that they had no power to harm us, even though they entered our skin. You may remember that we called the Anemone a cousin of the Jelly-fish, for they both belong to the same lowly division of the Animal Kingdom.

Animals have queer ways of getting a living. Who would expect to find millions of poisoned darts in a Jelly-fish? Who would guess that these weapons are coiled up, ready to spring out at their prey? Men have made many weapons for killing, from the bow-and-arrow to the torpedo, but none of them is more wonderful than the weapon of the Jelly-fish.

EXERCISES

1. Where is the mouth of the Jelly-fish placed?

2. How does the Jelly-fish move through the water?

3. What is the food of the Jelly-fish?

4. How does it obtain its food?

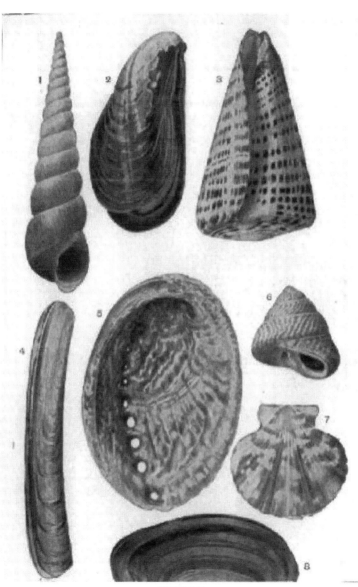

SHELLS

1. A FRESHWATER TURRET SHELL.

2. EDIBLE MUSSEL.

3. CONE SHELL.

4. SWORD-BLADE RAZOR-SHELL.

5. EAR SHELL, OR ORMER.

6. A TOP SHELL.

7. SCALLOP.

8. SWAN MUSSEL.

LESSON X.

SHELLS AND THEIR BUILDERS (1).

THE PERIWINKLE, WHELK AND LIMPET.

Most of the shells which you find scattered over the shore are empty. The little animals which built them are gone; and their empty houses, of wonderful shapes and colours, are all that you find. Let us look at the builders of these pretty homes.

The shell-builders have soft, juicy bodies, and they are put in one big division of the animal kingdom--the *mollusca*, which only means *soft-bodied*. Some of these molluscs do not build shells. But most of them build a shelly house for themselves; they do this to defend their soft bodies from the attacks of a host of enemies. Some build two shells--the Oyster and Mussel do, as you know. These are called *bi-valves*; that is, two valves or shells; and others, like the Garden Snail, the Limpet, and Periwinkle, have one shell only, and so are called *uni-valves*.

The crab, and other *crustaceans*, also have a hard covering to their soft bodies; but it is not at all like the shell of a Snail, or other *mollusc*. The Snail's shell is like the little boy's suit which is altered and made bigger as the boy grows. The crab's covering is a suit which cannot be altered. It must be thrown away, and replaced by a larger one.

The body of the shell-builder is wrapped in a soft covering, a kind of outer coat, which is called the *mantle*. Now this mantle is one of Nature's cleverest inventions. It is able to take the substance called *lime* from the food of the animal, and to use it as building stuff.

PRECIOUS WENTLETRAP.

The shell is built to fit the soft body. When a Periwinkle is hatched from the egg, it is as big as a pin's head. It eats and grows, and the shell must therefore be made larger. So the mantle is stretched out, and it puts a film of lime to the edge of the shell. Bit by bit the shell is thus added to by the wonderful mantle. Look at a snail's shell, and notice the lines which show how many times the little house has been made larger.

Each kind of shell-builder has its own style of building. If you go to a museum and examine the shells gathered from all over the world, you are surprised at their wonderful shapes, markings and colours. Another surprising thing is their size. Some are enormous, so large that they make good washing-basins. Others are so small that you can hardly see them. Each one was made by the folds of the mantle of the animal that lived in it.

In our coloured pictures you see many different kinds of shells, some of them built by uni-valve molluscs and some by bi-valve molluscs.

Wherever there are weeds along the shore you can find whole armies of the Periwinkle--the "Winkle" we all know so well. It browses there, among the weeds, just as its cousin, the land Snail, browses on your cabbages. You must have seen the little door with which the Periwinkle closes the entrance to his house. The land Snail does not own a door, but he makes one when he goes to sleep for the winter.

The Periwinkle crawls on a broad, slimy foot, which is put out from the shell. It is stretched on this side or that, and so draws him and his home in any direction. There are two sensitive feelers in front of his head; and behind these are two short stalks, on each of which is a tiny eye. If alarmed, the Periwinkle can shorten his body, and pull it back into its shell, closing the entrance with the horny door.

But the strangest part of him is the tongue. It is not for tasting, but for rasping. It is like a long, narrow ribbon, on which are hundreds of tiny points, all sloping backwards. They are arranged three in a row. The Periwinkle rasps the seaweed with his tongue, and so scrapes off his dinner. Of course the teeth wear away.

COWRIES.

But only part of the toothed ribbon is used at a time, so there are plenty of teeth behind the worn ones, ready to take their place.

The shell, as we have seen, is made of *limestone*. But the teeth are made *of flint*. This is a hard substance, so hard that it is used for striking sparks.

Now we will look at a shell-builder, the Whelk, who uses his flinty tongue in quite another fashion. The Whelk does not care for a vegetable dinner. He prefers to eat other molluscs--he is carnivorous, a flesh-eater; but these other molluscs do not wait to be eaten. As the enemy draws near they retire into their shells, and shut themselves up as tight as they can. The Whelk, however, is a clever burglar; he knows how to make a way into the hardest of shelly houses.

His front part--we might call it a nose--will stretch out to a fine point; and it contains a rasping tongue even harder than that of the Periwinkle. He sets to work. Moving the rasp up and down, he drills a neat round hole in the shell of the animal he is attacking. No shell is safe from him; and no tool could make a neater hole.

When you next gather shells on the beach, look at them closely; in some you will see where Mr. Whelk, the burglar, has been at work. He needs but a small entrance to enable him to suck out his helpless prey at his ease. Is it not strange that this creature, with a body as soft as your tongue, should earn its living by breaking into houses made of hard shell!

There are other molluscs which find their meals in this strange manner, and many others which, like the Periwinkle, feed more easily on seaweed. One of these, the Limpet, you can always be sure of finding at low tide; indeed, there are so many Limpets on the rocks that it would be hard *not* to see them. You will know, if you have tried to force a Limpet from its hold on the rock, how very tightly it clings. It is as if the shell were glued or cemented by its edges.

Yet there is no glue or cement used, but only a simple dodge. The Limpet has a broad "foot," which almost fills up the opening of its shell. Like the foot of the Snail, it is used when the animal wishes to take a walk; but it serves another purpose too. It can be used as a sucker; and it is this which enables the Limpet to cling so firmly to its rock.

When the tide is out, the Limpet clings to the rock, its soft body tucked safely away in the shell. Its feeding time comes when the water covers the rocks once more. Then the Limpet's shell may be seen to tilt up, and a foot, and a head with feelers and eyes, come out. The Limpet crawls to the seaweed and begins to browse, using a rasp like that of the Periwinkle. It then crawls back to its own place on the rock. In time this resting-place becomes hollowed out, and the Limpet's shell fits into the groove thus made.

Limpets are useful as bait for fish. The Whelk and Periwinkle are gathered in immense numbers, and are used by us for food. Perhaps you have seen the egg-bundle of the Whelk. It contains many eggs when first laid in the sea. Each egg is as big as a pin's head. They swell in the water, until the yellowish bundle is three times as large as the Whelk that laid it. You often see the empty bundle blown by the wind along the shore.

EXERCISES

1. Give the names of two bi-valve molluscs.

2. What is the Periwinkle's shell made of?

3. Describe how the Periwinkle eats seaweed.

4. How does the Whelk obtain its food?

5. Give the names of three one-shelled molluscs.

LESSON XI.

SHELLS AND THEIR BUILDERS (2)

THE MUSSEL AND OYSTER.

As everyone knows, the Mussel and the Oyster live between two hinged shells. In the last lesson we called them *bi-valve molluscs*, which is only another way of saying "soft-bodied animals with two shells." Have you ever opened an Oyster? It is a tug-of-war, your skill and strength against the muscles of the animal inside the tight shells.

Like the Periwinkle and other shell-builders, these creatures owe their strong houses to a wonderful *mantle*; but in this case the mantle is in two pieces instead of one. You can imagine the Periwinkle's mantle as a tube enclosing the animal's body. The mantle of the Mussel or the Oyster is in two pieces; and each half forms its own shell.

The Snail, and other one-shelled molluscs, poke their heads out of the shell when feeding or moving. Oysters and their two-shelled cousins cannot do this, for the simple reason that they have no heads!

In some places you see that the rocks at low tide are covered with Mussels. In dense black masses they cling to the rocks; and, though heavy waves bang them like so many hammers, they stick tight. Little Mussels and big ones, they form a mass so thick that baby crabs and other creatures use them as a hiding-place. On the piers and groynes, and the woodwork of the harbour, you can see other clusters of Mussels; they are placed where the high tide covers them.

Have you noticed how the Mussel anchors himself? He uses a bunch of threads, like so many cables or tiny ropes. It is interesting to know how these threads are made.

The Mussel is, as a rule, a stay-at-home, but he can move from place to place if he likes. He has a long, slender foot which can be pushed out of the shells. Now the threads are fixed by the foot, just where the Mussel wishes to anchor himself. They are made from a liquid which forms in the body of the creature. This liquid hardens in the water so that it can be pulled out into long, fine threads.

Our ordinary Mussels do not make very long threads, but those of some kinds are so long that they can be woven into silky purses or stockings. The Mussel which makes such long anchor-threads might be called "the silkworm of the sea."

If the Mussel is such a stay-at-home, how does he find his food? The answer is, that the food comes to him, brought by the ever-moving water. There are countless specks floating in the sea, mostly specks of vegetable stuff. These settle on the floor of the sea, just as dust settles on our house-floors; and the waves wash this "sea-dust" hither and thither. The Mussel or Oyster, with shells gaping wide open, is bound to get some of this food with the water which enters the shells.

The Oyster has no "foot," and is fixed in one place nearly all its life. It is an interesting animal; and one of such value as food, that hundreds of thousands of Oysters are reared in special "beds," and sent to the market at the proper season. Our British Oysters were famous even in the time of the Romans; they were carefully packed and sent to Rome, and, at the Roman feasts, surprising quantities of them were eaten.

Many sea-animals have wonderfully large families, but the Oyster, with its millions and millions of eggs, beats most of them. Strangely enough, its eggs are not sent into the sea at once, but are kept between the Oyster's shells until they hatch. Needless to say, these babies are very small indeed, else their nursery could not contain them all Though so small that thousands of them together look more like a pinch of dust than anything else, yet each one has two thin shells; so that, if you eat the parent Oyster, they grate on your teeth like sand. Oysters, at this time, are "out of season"--that is, unfit for food.

At the right moment, the Oyster gets rid of its numerous family. It opens its shells, then shuts them rapidly; and, each time this happens, a cloud of young Oysters is puffed out like smoke. Now these mites must fend for themselves in a sea full of foes.

They have no defence, and countless numbers of them are gobbled up by crabs, anemones, and others. If this did not happen, the sea would soon be paved with Oysters.

For a time, the baby Oysters--which are known as "spat"--are able to swim here and there. In rough weather they are driven far into the deeps of the ocean, and lost. The rest of them, before they have been free for two days, settle on the bed of the sea--sometimes on their own parents; and there they remain for life. Only a very few out of each million become "grown-ups"--the rest are eaten by enemies, or smothered in mud or sand. In a year or so they are as big as half-a-crown. In five years they are fine, fat grown-up Oysters--that is to say, if they have not been dredged up from their bed and sent to market.

Their shells open and shut like a trap. You may have seen a picture of an inquisitive mouse trapped by an Oyster. Thinking to have a nice taste of Oyster, the mouse had poked its head into the open shells, but they were snapped together, and the mouse was firmly held in the trap.

Between the hinge of the two shells there is a pad, which acts like an elastic spring, and forces the shells open. The Oyster can close them by means of a strong muscle. They are its only defence, so it closes them at the least hint of danger.

Even these thick walls are sometimes of no avail, as we saw in our talk on "Five-fingered Jack." We saw how the starfish forces the shells open with the help of its strong tube-feet. The whelk and his cousins know how to bore a hole in the shell, and suck out the helpless Oyster. Then there are certain sponges, with the strange habit of making holes in shells, and living in and on them. Sometimes the Oysters are stifled in their "beds" by other Oysters settling and growing over them. Thick masses of Mussels may cling to them and suffocate them. And grains of sand sometimes get in the hinges of their shells, so that they cannot close up the house when they wish.

Like the other animals which are useful as food, Oysters have been carefully studied and cultivated by man for many, many years. The story of the Oyster-beds is a long and interesting one.

Oysters feed in rather a strange way. You may have looked inside the shells and seen two delicate dark-edged fringes, known as the "beard." This fringe is the Oyster's gills or breathing arrangement. Trace the "beard" as far as the hinge of the shells, and you see the mouth with its white lips. If you could watch the creature having its dinner, you would see a constant stream of water flowing over the gills and towards the mouth.

What makes the water move in that way? The gills are covered with very tiny lashes, like little hairs. There are so many of them that, as they keep moving, they force the water along, over the gills and towards the mouth. In this way the Oyster breathes the air which is in the water; but not only that. As we have already noticed, there is a kind of "vegetable dust" in the sea. This is driven to the Oyster's mouth and swallowed. The Oyster, fixed in its "bed," unable to hunt for food, thus makes its dinner come to it. What a strange use for a "beard"! It not only serves as lungs, but also helps the animal to catch its "daily bread"!

Another mollusc used as food is the Cockle, and its shell is one of the commonest found along the shore, especially near sandy places. It lives in sand, and can bury itself so quickly that you would have to use your spade with all your might in order to keep pace with this little shell-fish. Where Cockles have buried themselves you will see spurts of water and sand, showing where they are busy down below in the wet sand.

Besides being so skilful at digging, the Cockle is a first-rate jumper. If left on the beach, it jumps over the sand, towards the sea, in the funniest way. It is strange to see a quiet-looking shell suddenly take to hopping and jumping like an acrobat.

To perform this astonishing feat the Cockle makes use of its foot, which is worked by very strong muscles. It is large and pointed, and bent: if the Cockle wishes to move quickly, it stretches out its foot from between the shells, as far as it will go. Then, by using all its power, it leaps backwards or forwards in a surprising manner.

There are many other interesting molluscs, besides those we have looked at. The Piddock, or Pholas, is a smallish, rather delicate one, with a soft foot. But this foot is a most wonderful boring tool, fitted with a hard file. Hard rocks and wood are perforated by these little molluscs. Indeed, they are a positive danger, for they pierce the wooden piles of piers, and weaken them. They cannot pierce through iron, however, and so iron plates or nails are used to protect the piles from their onslaughts. You will often see stones and rocks riddled by the Piddock as if they were as soft as cheese. Chalk, sandstone, or oak, it is all the same to the Piddock, which rasps them away with its file. When the points of this strange instrument are worn out with all this hard wear, a new set takes their place.

EXERCISES

1. How does the Mussel anchor itself?

2. Describe how the shells of the Oyster are opened and closed.

3. What is the food of the Mussel?

4. Of what use is the "beard" of the Oyster?

5. Why is the Oyster called a bi-valve?

6. Why is the Oyster sometimes unfit for use as food?

Printed in Great Britain
by Amazon